Only A Rake Will Do

Christina Diane

Only A Rake Will Do

Copyright 2024 by Christina Diane

Edited by Emily Lawrence

Cover Design by Devin McCain @studio5twentyfive

eBook ISBN: 978-1-964713-07-6

Paperback ISBN: 978-1-964713-09-0

ONLY A RAKE WILL DO

Contents

Dedication

For those of you that get excited when a spectacled bookish guy
is also a beefcake with a naughty side.

Note to Readers

I am so delighted and honored that you have picked up my book! Before you dive in, I would like you to know that I write for the modern reader. My stories are character-driven, fast-paced, and spicy with fun dialogue. While I love the Regency era and exploring the social constructs for the time period, I don't focus on complete historical accuracy. I complete research and attempt to create the setting and behaviors that are close to what you would expect of the era, but sometimes the characters and story have minds of their own. I wouldn't want you to be disappointed if you want a setting, themes, and language that are entirely accurate. If that is really important to you, this book might not be for you. And I understand!

Historical stories are a form of escape and are a fantasy in their own right, and I aim to help bring you to a world that might look and feel very much like the Regency era with diverse, inclusive characters who are fun, sexy, and intriguing as they find their path to love.

If you are excited about hard-headed and swoon-worthy gentlemen, spirited and passionate heroines, fun banter, high spice, and guaranteed happily ever afters, set in my interpretation of the Regency era, then I hope you will keep reading and escape into a world of passion, romance, and sharp tongues.

Content Warnings

While this book isn't heavy on content warnings,
I do my best to capture things that I think a
concerned reader might wish to know about. If
you ever feel like I missed something, please message me and I will update this list to improve
the reading experience for other readers. To prevent spoilers, you can find content warnings for all
of my published books here: https://christinadiane-
books.com/content-warnings/

Chapter One

Sussex, England Late - February 1812

Grace Armstrong, the youngest daughter of the Earl of Snowdon, rushed away from her brother's study after walking in on something she didn't understand between her brother, Elias, and his wife, Lydia. She only wished to ask her brother something, but she knew enough to know she would intrude if she interrupted whatever had made them so enamored with each other.

She raced away and found her sister Jenny in their parlor. "Sister, why would Elias enjoy Lydia sitting on his lap so much? Wouldn't he rather her sit in her own chair?" she asked, not pausing long enough for her sister to respond. "Perhaps it is easier to kiss her if she's in his lap, but still."

Jenny responded by laughing so hard her shoulders shook.

"What's so funny?" Diana, her oldest sister, asked as she glided into the room and sank into her usual spot on the plush settee.

"Grace entered Elias' study without knocking," Jenny said, laughing and flashing Diana a knowing look.

Grace was only three-and-ten and understood nothing that occurred between a husband and a wife. Her sisters gave each other that annoying look they reserved for when she was curious about things.

She wasn't convinced that Jenny, five-and-ten, or Diana, nine-and-ten, knew much more than she did. Girls weren't told much about what to expect, but as her older sisters, they acted as if they knew more than her on every topic.

"Oh my," Diana exclaimed. She poured cups of tea for both her and her sisters. "Dare I ask what you saw?"

The sisters were no strangers to stumbling upon Elias and Lydia in compromising positions throughout their sprawling country home. Grace was quite curious about the faint sounds of passion that echoed from behind closed doors from her brother and her sister-in-law. Not that anyone would explain it to her, even if she asked.

"Lydia was sitting on his lap, and they were kissing, so I ran away. He seemed to enjoy it far too much for me to interrupt. Don't enter any rooms in this house without knocking first," Grace said, releasing a fit of giggles.

"They are newlyweds. It's to be expected, I think," Diana said.

"I can't wait until I have a husband and get to kiss him all the time," Grace said dreamily. It was true. She couldn't wait to experience her first kiss.

"Are there any other qualities you would seek in a husband?" Diana asked. "Besides one that you wish to kiss."

Grace giggled. "Handsome and a good kisser!"

"Grace! You will want to look deeper than their appearance and kissing abilities," Diana said. "But you have a good start." Her sister winked at her.

Jenny set her cup down. "Tell us your list, Diana," she said. "What are you hoping for in a husband?"

"Well," she began, "I desire a husband who not only values my opinion but actively involves me in decisions concerning our estates. He must possess unwavering faithfulness and a genuine desire to be a devoted father to our children, just as Papa was to us."

"You didn't mention love in your list of requirements. Shouldn't that also be on your list?" Jenny asked.

Grace mentally added 'love' to her list. *Handsome, good kisser, love.*

"It would be preferable but so rare amongst *ton* marriages. I must be practical," Diana said. "And I must find a husband this season."

Jenny arched her eyebrow. "Right. Isn't that the point of the season?" she asked. "I don't understand."

"But I didn't find a husband last season," Diana said.

"You didn't try to find a husband last season, sister," Jenny countered.

"How would you know?" Diana asked. "What do you know about finding a husband when you aren't even out yet?"

Grace looked between her sisters, enjoying the exchange. She wanted to be just like them. Diana would leave for Town for the London season soon, and

Grace dreamt of the day she would make her own come out and meet all the handsome, interesting gentlemen. She sighed.

"I wager I know more than you, sister," Jenny said. "I know one must have prospects and interest in a gentleman if they intend to marry. You never mentioned a single gentleman last season. Did you even discuss any prospects with your friends?"

"Well, no," Diana replied. "But is it my fault that so many of the gentlemen are dreadful bores?"

Grace found it hard to believe that the men were boring. "There isn't a single gentleman you have found interesting?" she asked. She would find them all so interesting, especially the handsome ones.

"Not really," Diana replied. "I guess I didn't get to know that many gentlemen other than Elias' friends and they would never suit. Matt and Hudson are like brothers, and Jude is the biggest rake of the *ton*, even worse than Elias used to be."

"What is a rake?" Grace asked.

Diana and Jenny burst into whoops.

"What?" she asked. "Tell me!" They always thought she was too young to know things, and it drove her mad. She must prepare herself for the day she would take a husband, too.

Jenny stopped laughing after Grace cast her an annoyed glance. "It's a gentleman who likes to kiss ladies," Jenny replied. "And I'll leave it at that."

"Oh!" Grace exclaimed, pleased that her sisters gave her any information at all. "Well, that doesn't sound bad. Perhaps I would like a rake." She held her chin high. Her sisters must see her as a young lady and not a girl, eventually.

"Grace!" Diana said, glancing towards the door. "Never speak such a thing in front of Elias or Papa, or they will never allow you to attend the season!"

"I heard Lydia telling one of her friends that rakes make the best husbands," Jenny offered, shrugging her shoulders.

"Well, I should think one would want their hus-band to enjoy kissing them," Grace said. "I know I would."

"What do you know about kissing, Grace?" Diana asked.

She sipped her tea before answering, annoyed that her sister assumed she knew nothing at all. "Only what I read in my romance novels, which leaves me quite frustrated at how little they explain."

"I quite agree, sister," Jenny said. "I don't understand why no one will tell us about what one does when they are married. How will we be any good at it if we don't know what it is?"

"Perhaps Lydia will tell us," Diana said.

"Do you think Mama would have told us if she were here?" Grace asked. She didn't remember their mama, since she had been only a baby when she passed. She always enjoyed hearing the memories Elias and Diana could recall, even if she longed to recall stories of her own.

"I think she would before we married, as most mamas do," Diana said.

"If rakes make the best husbands, then Mama would tell us to marry a rake, right?" Grace asked.

Jenny burst into whoops again. "I'm not sure if she would use those exact words, sister."

"Why not?" Grace asked. "It sounds to me like what I need to look for in my husband." She pondered that for a moment and then nodded, deciding. "I shall set my cap on a handsome rake."

A voice bellowed from the doorway, "What did you just say?"

All three sisters turned their heads to see their brother and their sister-in-law standing there. Elias' expression bordered on murderous, while Lydia covered her mouth to hide her laughter.

Elias scowled at Jenny and Diana. "What have you two been telling your sister?"

Grace raised her chin. "I believe I am old enough to know such things, brother, and I know that when I marry, I want a handsome man who enjoys kissing, just like a rake."

Their brother choked and stepped further into the room. "I don't want to hear any more about rakes from any of you." He stared them down with the 'intimidating older brother' look he'd given them for years, which, unfortunately for him, had lost its effectiveness.

"My love, why don't you join your father and allow me to handle this?" Lydia patted his arm.

Grace scooted to the edge of her seat, hopeful Lydia might share more of the information she sought.

He shook his head before glancing at each of his sisters. "All right. But please put an end to all this rake talk."

"Do you not want us to speak of rakes because you are one, brother?" Grace asked, tilting her head to the side as she assessed her brother. Lydia certainly seemed to enjoy his kissing.

If Elias' eyes widened any further, they might have popped. "Who said I was a rake?"

Grace looked at Diana but said nothing. Elias shot a warning glance at Diana, but she hid her laughter behind her hand. He opened and closed his mouth, trying to find his words.

"Aren't you going to find your father now, my love?" Lydia asked. "I have this well in hand." She offered him a small smile, nodding towards the door and urging him to leave.

He sighed. "Very well. I hope when I see you all later, we have moved on to acceptable topics of conversation." He placed a kiss on Lydia's temple and exited the room. Grace smiled at them, thinking about what it might be like to have a man who adored her as much as her brother adored his wife. From the stories she had been told, her parents were quite the love match, too.

Lydia closed the door behind him before joining Diana on the settee. She nodded towards the tea, and Diana poured a cup for her.

"Now, sisters," Lydia started. "Some of what you say is true. Your brother was considered quite the rake in the scandal sheets before we were married."

"He must still be a rake if he enjoys kissing you so much," Grace said. Lydia eyed her curiously, but Grace continued, "Jenny said a rake is a gentleman who likes to kiss ladies, and Elias certainly seems to like it a lot."

The blush rose to Lydia's neck. "Well, that is true, and he does. A rake is a bit more than that, Grace. It is a man who is known for their experience with women."

"Is that why you said that rakes make the best husbands?" Grace asked.

Lydia choked but recovered. "Well, the experience they have is desirable for a husband."

Grace furrowed her brow. "What kind of experience?"

Each of the sisters leaned closer, eagerly awaiting Lydia's response.

"Well, experience that is important for marital relations. It's something husbands and wives do to make a baby." Lydia looked at her teacup, her expression tense.

"Is that what you were doing on Elias' lap in his study? Making our new niece or nephew?" Grace asked. The couple told them all at dinner last night that they were expecting a babe.

The whoops poured from Diana and Jenny, and Lydia turned the deepest shade of pink. Grace wasn't sure why it was so funny. How would she know how a baby was made if she didn't ask?

"We made our precious babe before then, Grace," Lydia said, placing a hand on her stomach. "I shan't tell you exactly what occurs until closer to your wedding, but I will tell you more about it when that time comes." Lydia took a sip of her tea before continuing, "And please, do your best not to speak of such things where your brother or father can hear. Just come to me with your questions."

The sisters nodded their agreement.

Lydia set her cup on the table and stood. "I shall see to your brother."

"Are you going to sit on his lap again?" Grace asked. Lydia just shook her head and hurried away, laughing. It seemed like a fair question to her.

At least she learnt more about what her list of requirements for her future husband would be. *Handsome, good kisser, love, rake.*

Chapter Two

London, England - Spring 1817

G race could hardly believe that she would experience her first season. She had dreamt of the balls and events she would attend. As soon as she arrived in town, she began reading the scandal sheets. She must know who all the rakes were, so she might form her list of potential suitors. She replayed her list of requirements in her head so many times. Handsome, good kisser, love, rake.

Diana and Jenny had both married, and both were love matches. They both had started their families and were quite content, indeed. It was her turn to experience the things her sisters didn't give her enough details about. She had a better idea now about how a husband and wife joined thanks to what little her sisters had shared, but she didn't understand how being a rake would impact what occurred. To her knowledge, her sisters hadn't married rakes.

Diana married Graham, the Earl of Powis, and Grace recalled he was quite dreamy when she first met him. Diana and he were still so enamored with each other, but he hadn't been a rake. Jenny married Thomas, one of the Duke of Bedford's sons. They were also constantly kissing and displaying the affection of their love match, but he also hadn't been a rake.

She would beat both of her sisters when she won a rake and would have the most passionate marriage of them all. No more could they treat her like their little, inexperienced sister. Not that they were ever unkind to her. She knew they loved her dearly, just as she did them, but something about being the youngest sister left her trying to get out from behind their shadows so she could shine all on her own.

Her maid finished styling her blond hair for her very first ball. "It looks perfect, Marie," Grace exclaimed. She was practically bouncing in her seat. Diana didn't marry until her second season, but she met Graham at the very first ball then. Perhaps Grace would find such luck and meet her future husband tonight.

She selected a blue ball gown since it accentuated her azure blue eyes that she and her siblings were all known for.

There was a knock at her door, then Lydia and Diana entered.

"Dearest, you look lovely," Diana said, stepping behind Grace in the mirror.

"Thank you," Grace replied. She felt quite beautiful. No longer the younger sister who had to remain in the country while her sisters experienced all that society offered. The *ton* wouldn't know what hit them.

Lydia smiled at her. "There is just one more thing you need," she said, presenting the most beautiful diamond set Grace had ever seen.

"I get to wear these tonight?" Grace asked.

"These were your mama's," Lydia explained. "Your sisters wore this set for the first balls of the season and their weddings." She clasped the necklace around Grace's neck. "And now it is your turn."

Diana affixed the bracelet on Grace's wrist. She noted how Diana tenderly touched the bracelet. It was the very piece of jewelry that aided in bringing her and Graham together, so it was special, indeed. Grace was honored to wear the set tonight. She handed Grace the earrings to adorn for herself.

Once she had the jewelry in place, Grace looked at herself in the mirror again. She sparkled. She bit her bottom lip, tamping her excitement over what the evening might hold.

"Are you ready to depart?" Diana asked.

"Very much so," Grace replied. "I wish Jenny could be here."

Lydia looped her arm through Grace's. "She does, too, dearest." Her sister was too far along with child to make the trip.

The trio departed Grace's chamber to make their way downstairs. She was staying with Elias and Lydia at their family townhouse, while Diana and Graham took up residence at their own townhouse, which was only a couple of blocks away.

Elias had grumbled about coming to town for the season. He had grown accustomed to spending more time in the country with his family. Grace's papa never came to town, preferring to remain in the country where he felt closest to their dear, departed mama. He would only venture to town if she were to select her husband this season.

Her brother and sister each brought their children with them for the season so they wouldn't have to be apart from them for months. It kept things interesting and full of life in the family townhouse. She adored all of her many nieces and nephews and looked forward to having her own children to add to the ever-growing bunch.

"You look beautiful, sister," Elias said as soon as they joined him at the bottom of the stairs. "And you as well, my love," he said to Lydia, then kissed her temple.

"And I find you to be the most beautiful of all," Graham said to Diana, taking her in his arms.

Grace snickered. Her family set the bar high for tenderness and affection in a marriage. The man for her would be the picture of romance and passion, sweeping her off her feet right away. Every lady of the *ton* would desire him, yet she would be the one to win his heart.

Grace glanced around the ballroom, taking in the sights of all the handsome gentlemen. The ballroom set the stage for the most romantic backdrop she had ever seen. The candles and music made for the perfect venue for her to fall in love with a handsome rake.

Many men had already signed her dance card, while her brother assessed each of them from behind her. She was fortunate that so many dared to approach their group. Almost everyone she knew while growing up stood nearby. All of her brother's and sister's friends, along with their spouses. It was overwhelming to have everyone tittering about the gentlemen and giving her their opinions. But little did they know she didn't need their help. She had a list and soon she would have her match.

"Grace." A familiar male voice caught her attention. "Might you have a dance available to partner with me?"

"Arthur," she replied, grinning at him. "It's good to see you again. Of course, here." She held up her wrist so he could pencil his name on her dance card. She met him a few months ago when he came for an extended visit over the holidays at Graham and Diana's country home. All the group in attendance tonight had gathered there to spend the holiday together, and he had accompanied his sister, Marina, and her husband, Evan.

"I look forward to our dance," he said, bowing to her. He departed and repositioned himself at Evan's side.

She had quite enjoyed his company when she met him. Arthur was extremely smart and loved talking about all that he learnt in his university days. He was far more scholarly than was typical of an earl. He even wore spectacles, which made him appear even more attractive. They spent many days exploring the library, and he never once tired of her asking questions. He answered her in detail and asked her questions about her interests. It was refreshing compared to how her siblings treated her.

Grace partnered with many gentlemen throughout the evening. With each one, she awaited the spark of attraction to hit her and confirm for her which one would be her husband. As the evening went on, she became more frustrated. So far, none of the gentlemen held her interest beyond polite conversation and mindless questions about her interests or the weather, even the ones known to be rakes.

She tapped her foot under her ballgown, releasing her anxious energy. How could she find the perfect love match to compete with her sisters if none of these gentlemen could even hold an interesting conversation?

"I believe it is our dance, my lady," Arthur said, holding his hand out to her. She hadn't noticed he had approached.

Grace took his hand, and he placed it in the crook of his arm. She was surprised at how large and firm his bicep was compared to some of the other men she had danced with.

The first strains of a waltz sounded, and he wrapped his arm around her back, then took her hand in his. She placed her other hand on his shoulder and noted the bulk beneath his coat. Arthur didn't meet the requirements on her list, but any woman would take note of his broad shoulders.

They danced, and he moved far more gracefully than she had expected him to. He seemed far too scholarly and into his books to have even taken the time to learn to dance.

"How are you finding the season, Grace?" he asked.

"Different from what I expected," she said, deciding she could be honest with Arthur since he wasn't a prospective suitor.

"How so?" he asked with genuine interest.

"I figured I'd be in love by now and know who my husband might be," she said. "Yet, I am just as far from selecting a husband as I was while hidden away in my country home."

He smiled at her, his expression thoughtful. "Well, the evening isn't over, so perhaps you still have time."

"Perhaps," she responded. "Affection and passion seemed to hit swiftly for my sisters."

"I don't think love strikes the same way for every person," he replied. "But I wouldn't think it makes the outcome any less affectionate or passionate."

She thought to herself about what he said. She replayed her list in her head. *Handsome, good kisser, love, rake.* That was what she wanted, and to win a rake, there must be instant passion.

"How about you?" she asked, changing the subject. "Are you enjoying the season?"

He gave her a lopsided grin. "I am, indeed. Although there are far more interesting sights outside of London ballrooms."

"Like what?" she asked, anxiously awaiting his response.

"There are new exhibits at the museum," he said, and the excitement shone bright in his eyes.

She couldn't help but smile back at his joy. He really was quite handsome. "I enjoy going to the museum. I intend to visit while we are here for the season."

"Well, I would be honored if you would allow me to escort you," he said. "I would love to experience it through your eyes. Tomorrow, perhaps?"

"That would be delightful," she replied. "I accept. Who knows when my brother or sister will detach themselves from their spouses long enough to take me?"

He laughed, a hearty, rich laugh, and she noted the sparkle in his green eyes. His eyes complemented his dark chestnut hair. He was sure to attract a spouse this season if he were looking to take a wife. If only he met her requirements, as she did so enjoy his company. Perhaps she would have to pay attention and see if there was anyone she could think to introduce him to.

When their dance ended, he escorted her back to their group. "I shall pick you up tomorrow at ten o'clock," he said. "If that is agreeable to you."

"Ten is perfect."

Chapter Three

Arthur Osborne was completely and totally in love, and he was quite certain the woman of his heart hadn't a clue. He told Grace that love didn't strike the same for every couple, but it had struck him with an unrelenting shock from the moment he first met her.

He spent the entire holiday at Graham and Diana's, attempting to get to know her better, to confirm his feelings. Hoping she might see him and feel the same. She deserved to have a season, but he couldn't allow her to marry someone else. So there he was, attending the balls and events with only one hope: that Lady Grace Armstrong would fall in love with him and agree to be his wife.

She consumed his every thought. She was a siren, who called out to him in his dreams with her blond hair cascading down her back and her blue eyes tempting him to walk over the edge of the cliff, deeper and deeper into his love for her. The dreams stoked a fire within him, and he would have been embarrassed to admit that he took himself in hand that morning to ease the tension and prevent himself from making his move too soon.

He wanted to love her, worship her, pleasure her, and far more. Yet, he wasn't certain she saw him as anything more than just another member of their mutual friend group. She had agreed to go to the museum with him, which was certainly a start. He needed to help her see him as a suitor, a lover, a husband, and not only as a friend.

"What are you woolgathering about, brother?" Marina asked, joining him in the breakfast room.

"Nothing," he grumbled, staring at his plate.

She laughed. "Oooh, so it's something." She waved her finger at him before making her selections from the sideboard.

"Leave me alone," he pleaded. He loved his sister, and normally he relished their banter, but this was serious. He may not have another chance to win Grace's heart. She was the most beautiful woman of the entire *ton* and would have lines of men seeking her attention and attempting to steal kisses. While she was so much more than a pretty face to him. His heart was pained at the thought of one of society's rakes attempting to get their hands on her.

Marina only laughed harder, and he rolled his eyes. "Have you ever known me to leave you alone?" she asked.

"There is a first time for everything," he said. "Surely the renovations are almost complete with your townhouse, so you can move back there."

She waved him off. "So who is she?"

Evan entered the breakfast room. "Come now, love, leave the man alone."

"Thank you," Arthur said. "My sister knows not what she speaks."

This time Evan laughed. "Oh, your mood is most certainly about a woman," he replied. "I just believe your sister shouldn't tease you about it. All of us gents go through the agonizing pain of trying to win the heart of the woman we love. And you deserve to have your pain in peace."

"You brought your pain upon yourself, love," Marina said, smirking at him.

"And it all worked out in the end," Evan said, giving her a quick kiss. He shifted his attention back to Arthur. "So let that offer you a bit of hope."

He hated to admit he envied the love between his sister and her husband, who had become like a brother to him. He adored his niece and nephew, who occupied the nursery upstairs. As a man of almost four-and-twenty, he hadn't given marriage or children much thought until Grace descended the grand staircase at her sister's home on Christmas Eve and captured his entire being.

"Are you going to tell us who she is, brother?" Marina asked, taking her seat to his left.

"Fine," he started. "But if you interfere in any way, I shall never forgive you."

Marina placed her hand on her brother's arm. "Arthur, we named our son after you," she said, her tone full of nothing but love. "We may needle each other, but I only wish for your happiness."

Arthur took a deep breath. "I hope to win Grace."

"Yes!" Marina cheered, clasping her hands together. "It crossed my mind to attempt a match, but I am glad you came to heel on your own."

He huffed. "It is not me who needs to be brought to heel. I don't think she considers me an option."

"I am certain she does," Marina countered. "You just must make her see you as the charming man you are. Women love romantic gestures. Evan won my heart over a picnic."

Evan laughed, and Arthur caught the wide grins between them.

"I don't require any further details," Arthur pleaded. They gave him an idea, though. "Please excuse me. I must make a few plans before I pick up Grace for our outing."

He didn't wait for their response and hurried away to make his plans.

Chapter Four

G race spent longer than she should have selecting her dress for the outing with Arthur. She wasn't certain why she had, given that it was just a trip to the museum with a kind man. He wasn't a real contender to be her future husband. He was handsome, to be sure, and he could perhaps be a good kisser. Her cheeks flushed, thinking about what it might be like to kiss him, and she pushed the thought away.

Arthur was not a rake. He wasn't the type of man who would bring the passion that she wished for in her marriage. The passion that would put all the couples she was acquainted with to shame.

The knowledge that they would never suit took all the pressure off the day. She could just be herself and not worry about dissecting everything he said or worry about being the proper lady at all times.

She descended the stairs and followed the loud chatter that reached her ears from the base of the staircase. When she reached the family parlor, she covered her mouth to mask her laughter at the scene before her.

Arthur and Elias were on the floor, having a pretend tea party with her niece, Emily. The sweet little girl with her blond curls pretended to pour them tea and urged them to drink it. Both of the men obeyed with their pinkies in the air.

"I believe this is the most delightful tea I have ever had, my lady," Arthur said.

The way her niece beamed at him, if she were a young miss on the marriage mart, she would have just set her cap at Arthur Osborne.

Arthur noted Grace's entrance and smiled at her. He shifted his attention back to Emily. "Thank you for having me for tea. I must depart to escort your aunt to the museum."

Emily's expression turned to a sad pout.

Arthur stood and bowed to her. "But I would be delighted to have tea with you again soon."

The smile returned to her face, and the little girl beamed up at him. He winked at her and then crossed the room to greet Grace.

"My lady," he said, bowing to her. "You look lovely this morning."

"Thank you," she returned. "I am looking forward to a day at the museum."

Arthur grabbed a flower from a side table and handed it to her. "This is for you."

It was a single pink rose with a ribbon tied around the stem. Grace brought it to her nose and inhaled the sweet scent of the bloom. "This was very sweet of you, Arthur."

"Are you going to marry him?" Emily asked, watching the scene unfold.

Grace covered a cough and avoided looking at anyone in the room. Her brother snickered, and she fought the urge to hurl something at him.

"I would if I were you," Emily continued. "He's so handsome."

Grace regained her composure. "I shall take that under advisement, Em," she responded. She didn't wish to insult Arthur, especially when he wasn't intending to ask her to marry him.

"You, my little lady, are never leaving my sight," Elias said, tickling his four-year-old daughter.

Everyone had a hearty laugh over that.

"Shall we depart?" Arthur asked, extending his arm to her.

She took his arm and allowed him to escort her. She caught Smith, their butler, on their way out. "Will you put this in water and have it placed in my chamber?" she asked, handing him the delicate rose.

Grace wouldn't need to bring her maid along for the outing since they traveled in an open carriage and would attend the museum. It was one of the first times she had gone anywhere without some sort of chaperone, and the notion was thrilling.

Once they were outside, Arthur handed her into his carriage before he climbed in and took up the reins. Conversation came easily as Arthur navigated them to the museum. They shared stories about their families, some of Arthur's learnings, and books that Grace had read recently. Grace had a twinge of disappointment when they reached the museum since she had enjoyed their conversation so much.

He came around to her side of the phaeton and instead of handing her down, he clasped her waist with his large hands and brought her down to stand on her feet in front of him. She became more aware of the strength his broad shoulders carried and pushed aside the feelings it stirred within her.

She put her hand in the crook of his arm, and he escorted her inside the museum. They resumed their comfortable conversation as they navigated through the different exhibits. She read each of the plaques, and he told her of the extended study he had done in maths and physics. Grace found herself enamored with the rich baritone of his voice.

They must have been at the museum for at least a few hours, but it passed by in the blink of an eye.

"Would you like some refreshment?" Arthur asked.

"That would be delightful," she replied, realizing she was famished.

He led her to a staircase, and they climbed the stairs to a balcony that overlooked a section of the museum. There was no one else present, and they had it to themselves. She released him and looked out across the balcony. "You can see everything up here," she said. "Oh, and look up, you can see the detail of the architecture even better. Come here, Arthur, you must see this."

He was at her side, looking up at the scene with her. She became far more aware of his presence, and an intoxicating cedar scent took hold of her senses. He flashed her a lopsided grin, and her breath caught. Something sparked in her, but she drew a deep breath and ignored it.

"I have arranged for us to enjoy a light repast up here," he said, motioning to a table she hadn't noticed when they first arrived.

He seated her at the table and took his seat beside her, his thigh pressed against hers. It was impossible for her not to be acutely aware of his presence.

Arthur prepared a plate for her with a few of the small sandwiches and a lemon tart. He poured them each a glass of lemonade. They resumed their comfortable conversation, but she couldn't stop herself from noticing each of his masculine traits and wondering how soft his hair might be. When he licked crumbs off his bottom lip, she caught herself noting its fullness. Something heated in her, and she wasn't certain where it came from, only that it had never occurred before.

When they finished their meal, he clasped her hand and pulled her to stand. He led them away from the balcony, just out of sight from anyone who might see them.

"May I kiss you?" he asked, leaving her breathless.

She could only nod as she swallowed hard.

He placed his hands on her hips and pulled her closer to him, but maintained a respectful space between them. Leaning his head down, he pressed his lips to hers. The electricity of his lips against hers consumed her every sense. Something pooled and heated in her core, and she imagined him touching her in places she had never noticed before.

When he pulled away, she almost sported the same pout as little Emily. She longed for him to deepen the kiss, to show her the passion she had been dreaming of for years.

She masked her disappointment and smiled up at him.

"I had better return you home before your brother comes looking for you," he said.

Once they were settled back in his carriage, she was lost in her thoughts. He caught her attention when he said her name.

She looked over at him, waiting for him to speak again as he guided the horses.

"Would you allow me to court you, Grace?" he asked. She noted how hard it was for him to speak the words.

She thought about her list and what she wanted. The passion she wanted from the man who would become her husband. Arthur was handsome and a good kisser, and he stirred things in her. But could he be the other things for her, too?

"I'm uncertain that is a good idea," she replied.

"Oh," he said, disappointed. "Did you not enjoy our time together today?"

The hurt in his expression broke her heart, and she inclined herself to be honest with him. She didn't want him to believe he had done anything wrong.

"I enjoyed our time very much. It's just..." she said, trying to find the words.

"Just what?" he asked. "You can tell me."

She swallowed hard. "You are kind, thoughtful, and so very romantic."

"But," he said, encouraging her to state her concern.

"I have always pictured myself marrying a rake," she said, looking away from him. "It's on my list of requirements."

"A rake?" he asked. "Why on earth do you wish to marry a rake?"

"Lydia has always said that a rake makes the best husband. I want passion, and need, and intensity beyond what my siblings have found with their husbands," she said, sighing after she finished.

"I see," he said.

They pulled up in front of her home, and she hated that she had hurt his feelings. He was so good and kind, and she couldn't help but wonder if she had it all wrong. Had she built up her idea of what her future would be for so long, she had closed herself off from what was right in front of her?

He lifted her down from the carriage again, and her skin heated in the places where his hands touched her, and he didn't release her. She looked up at him, and a smirk played at his lips.

"Point out your chamber window to me," he said.

Without thinking, she pointed to indicate which one would lead to her room.

He leaned closer and whispered in her ear, "Leave it unlocked tonight."

She gasped, and dampness pooled between her thighs. She wasn't certain what it meant, but the notion of him appearing in her chamber tonight was thrilling. Silently, she cursed her sisters for not telling her more, even though they had each said they would.

Chapter Five

Arthur laughed to himself as he assessed how he would climb into Grace's window. He planned the perfect romantic outing with the woman he loved. When they kissed, he fought every urge to pull her against him, allowing her to feel the hard ridge in his breeches from the mere touching of their lips. Something primal would have taken over if he had allowed himself to succumb to anything more than a sweet kiss.

He didn't want to scare her away, and as he came to find out, his siren wanted exactly that. She wanted to be tempted and brought to the brink of pleasures she didn't even know existed yet. If she wanted romance mixed with wild, unbridled passion, she was in luck. It was all he hoped to find with her, too.

There was a lattice attached to the house, and he only hoped it would hold him. Her brother would kill him if he knew what Arthur attempted, but love made one do crazy things. He tested his footing and continued climbing the lattice, deciding he couldn't stop or look down. Once he reached the window, he found it unlocked and slid it open so he could climb inside.

He took in the room to find a low fire in the fireplace and a candle lit on a bedside table. His eyes focused, and he spotted her. She was ethereal in her white night rail. His heart caught in his throat seeing her thus, with her long blond hair in a loose plait over her shoulder.

"Arthur," she whispered, standing in the center of her room as if she had been pacing and waiting for him.

He closed the distance between them and swept her to him, then pressed his lips to hers with fervent need. When she parted her lips in surprise, he swept his tongue across her lips, exploring her until their tongues met. She sank into him and matched his movements, actively engaging in the intensity of their kiss. The hard ridge appeared again in his breeches, and he knew she felt it as he held her tightly against him.

When he broke the kiss, she panted and laid her head on his shoulder.

"I had no idea..." she started.

"That kissing could be so intense?" he asked, finishing her statement.

She nodded against him, still catching her breath.

He pulled her back so he could look into her eyes. Her eyelids were heavy with desire and she looked at him as if he were the only person who existed in her world.

"It's not like that with everyone," he said. "You must care deeply for and desire the other person for it to be so. That is how I wished to kiss you earlier today."

She looked up at him, and his heart flipped. He tucked a loose curl behind her ear.

"You said you wanted a rake," he started. "While my name has never been seen in the scandal sheets for bedding many women, could you perhaps be content with a man who loves and wants only you? Who feels such passion and desire for you that he'd climb into your window, risking death by fall or at the hands of your brother, to ensure you knew just how cherished you are?"

She swayed at his words, and a tear formed in the corner of her eye. Cupping her face, he wiped it away with his thumb and she nuzzled her face against his hand.

He leaned closer so his lips brushed her ear. "And if you want pleasure so intense you beg for more, I intend to give you that, too."

She grabbed the collar of his coats and pulled him closer to her, initiating another intense kiss between them. He gasped when she pulled off his cravat and kissed along his neck and jaw.

"Please," she whispered. "I need something."

He cupped her mons over her night rail. "Do you need it here?" he asked.

She nodded, releasing a low moan when he applied a bit more pressure there.

"And do you wish for me to be the one to give it to you?" he asked. He needed her to say the words. He needed to know that she had pushed aside the idea of some nameless rake and realized that she wouldn't be left wanting for anything as long as she had him.

"Yes, Arthur," she said. "Only you."

It was the only invitation he needed. Arthur scooped her into his arms and carried her over to her bed, then laid her down as if she were a precious piece of glass. He checked to make sure her door was locked and then shrugged out of his coats. He kicked off his boots and socks and climbed into the bed next to her, wearing only his breeches and shirt. His heart thumped in his chest, taking in the sight of her before him.

She began working the buttons of his shirt, and as soon as she had unfastened them all, she ran her hands along his chest. His breath caught and his muscles flexed beneath her soft fingers.

"I knew you would look like one of the Greek statues we saw at the museum," she said, continuing her exploration.

"So you imagined me without my clothes on?" he asked, amused.

"Perhaps," she said, raising her chin. "I wondered what such a scholarly man did to have these."

He shifted his hand to graze the top of her chest, dipping his fingers below the edge of her night rail. "It's true that I enjoy maths and learning, but I also help my tenants with work when needed. I find I very much like using my hands," he said, shifting his hand until he cupped one of her perfect breasts.

He ran his thumb over her nipple and smiled when she gasped. He shifted her night rail down to expose her chest to him and dipped his head to take one of her tight buds into his mouth. She arched her back, pushing her chest against him as he sucked and flicked her nipple with his tongue.

"Arthur," she moaned.

He responded by switching to her other breast. He groaned, enjoying how her skin had the faint taste of vanilla.

When he raised his head to meet her eye, she smiled at him, and his heart did a series of flips. "Do you wish for me to show you more?" he asked.

"Very much so," she whimpered. "Please."

"Show me where you believe I should touch next," he said, teasing her nipple with his thumb.

Her eyes widened for a moment before her desire took over and she ran a hand down her stomach and pulled up the hem of her night rail to expose her mound to him. Her fingers continued their exploration until she reached her most private place and pointed. "Here."

"Hmmm," he said, still lazily playing with her nipples. "I'm uncertain I know what you want. Why don't you touch yourself there and see if we can find the right place?"

"Are you making fun of me?" she asked.

He leaned down and kissed her lips and then her neck. "Never," he replied. "I very much want to watch you explore your own body, and then I shall have my turn." His cock could hardly stand to be contained, testing the integrity of his falls with every movement of her fingers closer to her core. But this was about her, and he would remain caged until the time was right.

She found the delicate pearl with her fingers and cried out. "What is that?"

"Keep going. Slide your fingers into your folds," he said, his tone low and gravelly.

Doing as he instructed, she pushed further and her finger disappeared. "It's wet," she said, her breath catching.

"Give me your hand," he instructed.

She removed her finger and brought it up to him, and he pulled her hand closer to him, taking her finger in his mouth. He sucked every bit of wetness from her finger and her head rolled back.

"You have choices, love," he said, lowering his head to kiss her again. After a few moments, he broke the kiss. "Do you wish to experience your first climax by your own hand, mine, or my mouth?"

"I...I..." she started.

He held his breath, knowing what he hoped she would pick, but he would honor whichever she wanted.

"Would it make me wanton if I said your mouth?" she asked.

"Would it make me a rake if I hoped that was what you would pick?" he asked, coming to his knees. He shifted so that he was between her legs. Still kneeling, he gripped her thighs and pulled them further apart.

He positioned himself lower so his face was only inches away from tasting the most perfect woman who had ever walked the earth. "So to be clear, you wish for me to use my mouth here..." He brushed his thumb in a circle around her nub.

She bucked beneath him and pushed herself against his hand. "God, yes."

He slid a finger inside of her heat. "And how about here?"

She rocked against his hand, moaning. "Arthur. Yes. Please." The words came out between moans.

After exercising the patience of a saint, he lowered his head and flicked her pearl with his tongue. Her hands shot to his head, and she held his head against her, rocking from his attention. He suckled her, which only made her buck harder. He slipped lower and pushed his tongue inside of her, lapping up all that she gave him.

Arthur licked his way back to her nub and inserted a finger inside of her while he worked his tongue, making her cry out.

"Cover your mouth, love," he said to her. "Unless you wish for your brother to duel me."

She did as he said, and he relished her muffled cries when he resumed his attention. He increased the pace of his finger until she bucked and shattered. The tightening and clenching of her core around his finger almost made him come in his breeches. She would be so tight wrapped around his cock, and he could only hope she'd grant him the honor of being the one to love her that way.

After she stilled, he shifted his tongue lower and drank from her, cleaning her climax away with his tongue.

When he had his fill, he shifted to lie beside her and pulled her to face him. He kissed her, allowing her to taste herself on his tongue and lips.

She broke the kiss and looked at him. He hoped what he saw was affection in her expression, but swallowed hard and attempted to guard his heart.

"That was wonderful," she said, brushing his hair away from his face.

The tenderness in her touch broke his resolve to hope for anything but a future together. Unable to speak, he just smiled at her and nodded.

"Is there something I can do for you, too?" she asked. "Do you feel as I feel?" She reached her hand towards his cock.

He grabbed her hand and held it against his chest.

"Tell me your list," he said. "Tell me your requirements for a husband."

Chapter Six

"Arthur, it doesn't matter any longer. I was mistaken." She didn't want to speak the vapid words to the man she realized was the most perfect man for her. He had been nothing but tender, romantic, and full of passion for her. He didn't make her feel like the silly little sister, and she didn't want to become that in his eyes.

Arthur shook his head. "Tell me," he softly urged.

She sighed and looked at their hands clasped against his chest. "Handsome, good kisser, love, rake," she said, realizing how shallow the words sounded out loud. They were a schoolgirl's list, and she had become a woman. She better understood the intimacy and connection between a man and a woman. What she felt for him, and what he said he felt for her, couldn't be forced, nor subjected to a list of requirements.

She braced herself for his response, but to her surprise, he didn't laugh or chastise her.

"Well," he started, "you tell me, but I think I'm passably handsome. Perhaps the spectacles aren't in fashion."

With a sudden urge, she kissed him softly on the lips. "They make you even more handsome," she whispered.

"You have experienced my work, so you can also decide if I am a good kisser," he said, leaning down and taking her lips again. Her toes curled from the intense invasion of his tongue massaging hers, still tasting a bit of the wickedness from when he had tasted between her legs.

When he pulled away, she grinned at him. "I don't have anyone else to compare it to," she said, smirking at him.

"Well, I shan't encourage you to go around kissing anyone else," he said, "so perhaps just take my word for it."

She nodded. "I am inclined to agree."

"Very well," he said. "So that brings us to the matter of love next. I fell in love with you over the holiday with our families. I suspected I could when I first saw you, and I knew I did at the quick ease we found conversation, our shared curiosity about the world, and the light that radiates from you."

Tears streamed down her face, hearing his voice crack on the last few words. That was the most romantic, perfect thing she could have dreamt a man would say to her.

She opened her mouth to speak, but he put her finger over her lips to stop her.

"Then there is your last requirement. A rake," he said. "That's a tricky one. I shall never be known to entice numerous women because my heart belongs to one. I am more than willing to experience every wicked thing your body desires and can introduce you to many ways to make you come in my arms, but does that make me a rake?"

Before she could reply, he started again. "The key difference between me and the rakes you have heard so much about is that I will take none of my own pleasure from you without the commitment that you are mine forever."

The tears streamed down her cheeks even faster. His words touched her in ways she hadn't even known were possible. He leaned down and placed a light kiss on her lips before cupping her face with both hands and wiping her tears away with his thumbs.

"I am going to speak to your brother tomorrow and ask for proper permission to ask for your hand," he said. "I don't want you to give me an answer now. I want you to think about what I have shared and what you want for yourself. I shall accept whatever you choose as I wouldn't wish for anything to diminish your happiness."

He kissed her again and climbed out of the bed. She wanted nothing but to grab him and pull him back.

"Arthur," she called after him as he buttoned his shirt.

He shook his head. "Tell me tomorrow," he said softly. "I need you to be certain."

She nodded, and he gave her the boyish half-grin that would melt her heart each and every time he did so.

He slid his arms into the sleeves of his coats and donned his socks and boots. He crossed the room back to the window and climbed out. Holding on to the sill from the outside, he spoke again. "Good night, Grace," he said. "And you might want to lock this window. You never know when some lovesick man might climb up here."

She giggled and jumped out of the bed, racing to give him one more kiss. She watched him climb down the lattice and held her breath until he was safely back on the ground. He bowed to her from the ground and in a matter of moments, he disappeared into the dark street.

She closed the window but didn't lock it. Even though she knew he wouldn't return that evening, she couldn't bring herself to turn the lock and remove the chance.

Grace returned to her bed and pulled the covers over herself. She struggled to find sleep, thinking about what she wished to say to Arthur when she saw him tomorrow.

Chapter Seven

Arthur had never been more nervous in his life. He had to take up an earldom at the age of eight-and-ten, denied the worst blackguard of the ton his sister's hand, and gave countless speeches and lessons during his time at university. But asking permission to marry the woman he loved from a man such as Elias was proving to set him on edge. Her brother stood between the chance to even ask her the question.

He realized he had made things far too easy on Evan and should have at least made him squirm a little. It would have only been fair after the way Arthur's stomach reeled, waiting for Elias to attend to him.

Then there was the matter of if she would even accept him at all. He'd worry about that once he faced her brother. He shook off his fears and watched the door of the study he had been shown to.

A few moments later, Elias swept into the room and shook his hand. "Arthur, good to see you. There was something you wished to discuss with me?" he asked. "I hope Evan and Marina are well."

Elias motioned for him to take the seat across from his desk before seating himself and clasping his hands across his waist, waiting for Arthur to respond.

"They are well. I am here to speak to you about Grace, my lord."

Elias leaned forward. "My lord, is it?" he asked, laughing. "I can assume where this is going."

"I wish to marry her," Arthur blurted out, releasing the breath he had been holding.

"Interesting. I don't recall being asked if you could court her. Is there something I should know, given the sudden request?" Elias asked, narrowing his eyes at him.

"I fell in love with her months ago," Arthur said. "I only took up the season to win her heart, and I believe she knows my character well enough to decide."

"And does my sister share your affections?" Elias asked. "Does she love you, Arthur?"

"I am unsure," he answered honestly. "I am certain she cares for me, but only she can confirm if love is what she feels." His heart clenched, hoping she did.

"Very well," Elias said. "You are a good man, Arthur. If my sister accepts you, I have no reason to withhold my permission."

Relief washed over Arthur that the first part of his battle was won. "Thank you, Elias."

"I look forward to welcoming you to the family," Elias returned.

"We must see if she accepts me first," Arthur reminded Elias, or more so reminded himself, in the event she declined his proposal.

"Would you like for me to ring for her now?" Elias asked.

Arthur nodded, swallowing hard. He patted his pocket where the ring he had selected for her rested, awaiting its rightful place on Grace's finger. Marina had been elated to help him select it from the family jewels.

Elias reached for the bellpull and asked Smith to have Grace attend them. Arthur struggled to get air to his lungs with each second that passed as he waited for her to arrive. Elias looked far too amused for his liking, and he fought not to roll his eyes.

When Grace finally arrived, all thought left his body. Both men stood. Every part of him was aware of her presence, and he attempted to read her reaction to him.

"I shall give you a few moments," Elias said, then pointed at Arthur. "But only a few, and nothing untoward."

Elias nodded to his sister before departing, closing the door behind him.

Arthur drew a deep breath and took a few steps closer to Grace. She held her hand up as if to stop him, and his heart caught in his throat.

"I wish to run through my list again before you speak," she said.

He nodded, his stomach in knots, waiting to hear what she would say.

"I thought more about how you stack up to my requirements," she started. "You are most certainly handsome. So much so that I believe many women would be quite jealous if you were to find yourself off the market."

He smiled at her and urged her to continue.

"I have done nothing but long for your kiss since you departed, and I never wish to have anyone but you kiss me. I am glad you are my first and wish for you to be my last."

He took another step closer, and she held up her hand again to halt him.

"I believed that love was only uncontrollable passion. I know now that love is so much more than that, something far deeper, but includes passion. Thinking back on things, I fell in love with you at our picnic at the museum. I suspected I could love you when you had a tea party with my niece, and I knew I did when you truly listened to what I had to say and answered my questions without making me feel like an impertinent little girl. You make me feel like a woman.

"As for my misguided notion of a rake," she continued, "all I know is that my entire body is consumed with wanting you. You. Not an idea of what I believed it might be. But if I am honest, you have already far exceeded anything I might have dreamt of."

He closed the rest of the distance between them, not giving her the option to stop him. He pulled her to him and lowered his lips to meet hers. Breaking their kiss, he dropped to one knee in front of her and held up the ring he had retrieved from his pocket. "Lady Grace Armstrong, will you please do me the honor of becoming my wife?"

"Yes!" she exclaimed, pulling him back to her. He slipped the ring onto her finger and kissed her again.

After several kisses, she pulled back. "Please forgive me for taking far too long to realize that my requirements were the musings of a girl. You are so much more than that silly list."

"You have nothing to apologize for," he said. "Perhaps you'll have a few new things to add to your list soon." He winked at her.

"Does that mean you will climb into my window again tonight?" she asked.

"My lady," he started. "With my ring on your finger, I shall do anything you wish." He leaned closer and whispered in her ear, "Anything."

"How soon can we wed?" she asked, looking up at him with so much love that his heart soared.

"I shall convince your brother to allow us to marry by special license, so we can do so right away," he replied, pulling her close to kiss her again. He'd never tire of kissing the woman who would be his wife.

Elias barged back into the room.

"Come on, Arthur," he commanded. "Time to go."

"Brother," Grace protested. "He is to be my husband. Don't pretend you and Lydia didn't steal more than kisses before you wed."

Elias groaned. "Which is why your groom and I are going right now to purchase a special license. Neither of your sisters could wait to wed, so I didn't expect you to be any different," he pretended to narrow his eyes at her and then smiled. "I've mellowed out a bit after going through this three times."

"What about when Emily is of age?" Grace asked, needling her brother.

Annoyance marred his expression. "Let us not speak of such things until I am required to. I don't wish to think of it."

Chapter Eight

G race laughed, watching Arthur work his way
into the window again. She bit her bottom lip
and waited for him to get safely on his feet before
closing the window behind him. "I was beginning to
think you weren't coming."

"Evan and Marina," Arthur said, rolling his eyes.
"They wouldn't leave me be so I could depart. They
are happy for us, at least."

"Well, you are here now, and I don't wish to waste
a second of it," she said, pushing him onto the bed
and climbing on top of him. She straddled her legs on
either side of his lap and pressed her lips to his.

"I shall require you to always greet me this way," he
said.

She kissed him again and noted the bulge between
his legs became harder against her core. Grace knew

enough from the little her sisters had shared that he would insert himself inside of her, but nothing of what it might feel like in her hand. She had only seen the marbles at the museum and they hadn't proved all that educational.

She rocked her hips on his lap, and he groaned.

"My love," he said, "I'm not too proud to admit that I shall spend if you continue."

"Will you feel the pleasure you gave me when you do so?" she asked, momentarily pausing her movement.

"Indeed," he said, lifting one of her breasts from her night rail and suckling her tight bud.

She rolled her head back, and he kissed her chest and neck.

"I want you, Arthur," she whispered. "I want all of you."

"I'm wearing far too much clothing," he said, placing kisses along the globes of her breasts.

She pulled off his cravat and unbuttoned his coats, then he helped her shrug himself out of them, tossing them aside. Working at the buttons of his shirt, she kissed his neck and trailed her kisses further down his chest as she exposed more of his muscular form. The shirt joined the other clothing on the floor. Reaching between them, she began working at the buttons of his falls.

He lay back and clasped his arms behind his head, watching her unwrap the package she was most delighted at seeing. His member sprang to life between them. She was enamored with it. She ran her fingers along it and enjoyed the way he reacted to each slight touch.

His large shaft was smooth to the touch, yet a solid rod when she fisted it with her hand. It protruded from a nest of dark curls. There was a bit of liquid that had formed at the tip, and she ran her finger over it before bringing her finger to her lips to taste the saltiness of it for herself.

"And this is supposed to fit inside of me?" she asked, running her hand along it again.

"Mmm," he moaned. "Yes, my love. And I assure you, it shall." She still wasn't so sure, but she trusted him to know.

He flipped her over onto her back. He kicked off his boots and socks, and she came up on her elbows to watch him shift his breeches down his hips and let them fall to the floor. Seeing his naked form, he put every marble statue to shame. She was a lucky woman, indeed.

Arthur climbed back on the bed and hovered over her. "Now you are the one who is overdressed," he said, kissing her before grabbing the side of her night rail and lifting her to pull it over her body.

"Much better," he said, placing a trail of kisses along her collarbone.

She wrapped her legs around him, and he teased her opening with his member, groaning when he did so.

"There is no turning back once we do this," he said. "I shall consider you married to me from this moment forward."

"Nothing on this earth could cause me to cry off from marrying you, my love," she said, wrapping her arms around his neck.

"There could be a babe," he said.

"It's a good thing I very much wish to carry your children," she said, kissing and sucking the corded muscles of his neck.

Arthur slipped his hand between them and slid his finger inside of her, groaning. "You are so wet and ready for me." He circled her nub with the same finger, the dampness of his finger sliding easily around the sensitive skin.

She dug her fingers into his back and tightened her legs around his waist.

He positioned himself at her opening. "This may hurt, sweetheart, but it should only be this time. I'll do my best to ease you into it."

She nodded and clung to him, awaiting whatever feelings his entry would bring. He slid himself in slowly, allowing only an inch at a time to enter her before he gave a final thrust to push the rest of himself inside of her. She winced, and he gave her a tender kiss. "I'm so sorry. It should feel better soon."

He remained still for a few moments, and she had the urge to shift against him. "Oh, Arthur," she cried out. He smiled down at her and began shifting his hips so that he thrust into her. Each time he fully seated inside of her, she moaned and pushed her hips to meet him.

"Do you like this?" he asked, almost pleading.

"More than I even knew to hope for," she said, shifting her hand to cup his cheek. "I love you." She had never felt closer to another person than she had in that moment, becoming one with him.

He thrust into her again. "I love you, too, sweetheart."

Increasing his speed, she panted and fought to catch her breath. He drove her to the most exquisite release, shaking and rocking against him as the ecstasy spread from her core all the way to her fingertips. He thrust himself deep inside of her and moaned her name, pumping himself into her with small thrusts.

Arthur fell beside her and his spectacles shifted off center on his nose. He straightened them. "I should have removed these."

She turned to face him and nuzzled her naked body against his. "Never remove them," she said, placing a few quick kisses on his neck and jaw. "I quite like them. Plus, I shall want you to see when I take my turn tasting you."

He bit his bottom lip, and she loved the effect her words had on him.

"It's an excellent thing we shall marry in three days," he said. "Because I'm not letting you leave our bed for at least a week."

"Make it two," she said, shifting her wicked hand between them.

Epilogue

2 months later

"Husband," Grace said, entering Arthur's study and closing the door behind her. "I thought I might find you here."

"I would welcome such a beautiful distraction," he said, tossing his quill on the desk and urging her to come and sit in his lap.

She rushed over to him and threw her arms around his neck, then took his lips in a searing kiss. Since they had been married, they still could hardly keep their hands off each other. She was wanton for her husband and sought him out whenever wicked thoughts crossed her mind.

"Did you need me for something?" he asked, kissing her neck.

"Indeed, my love," she pressed her lips close to his ear. "I wish to taste your cock."

His bulge became rock hard against her hip, and he released a low growl.

"Does that mean you are agreeable?" she asked, shifting herself to kneel before him.

He worked his falls and released himself, then stroked his shaft a few times in his hand. "What do you think?"

She waved his hand away and took control, reveling in the way he moaned and rocked in his chair. Fisting his cock, she licked and sucked around the tip while stroking him. She slowed her hand and took more of him in her mouth. She took as much as she could, the head tickling the back of her throat.

Looking up at her husband, she sucked hard. He met her gaze and when she swallowed deep, his head fell back and he rocked his hips with her movements. She enjoyed studying him to learn what brought him the most pleasure and teasing his climax out of him. Grace also knew that this performance would earn her a delightful reward later, and her thighs were wet from anticipation.

His cock grew hard as stone in her mouth and his warm seed hit her tongue, and she swallowed it down, sucking every drop of his climax from him until he became still to catch his breath.

Remaining on her knees, she helped tuck him back into his falls and buttoned them.

"Arthur, Grace. Oh..." Marina said, barging into the room.

Grace rose from the floor and sat on Arthur's knee, laughing. "We are at least finished this time."

Relief washed over Marina's face.

"Sister, will you ever learn to knock?" Arthur whined.

Marina planted her hands on her hips. "The doors have locks. You could try using them."

"You have your own townhouse," Arthur spouted back. "You could try living there."

"We are moving home tomorrow," she replied, waving him off. "I seem to recall you telling Evan and me you didn't wish to catch us groping each other when we married."

"Yes," he replied. "In my house. I don't care what you do in your house. But this"—he waved his hands—"is our house. Besides, we're newlyweds, and you are an old married couple with children."

Marina laughed. "I'm only one year older than you are, and my husband has taken me twice already today."

"Sister!" Arthur shouted.

Grace patted her husband's shoulder and stifled her laughter. She had always thought her sisters had been spirited in their banter, but Arthur and Marina were a sight to behold. They were the best of friends and knew how to get under each other's skin.

"Don't call us an old married couple, then," she said, rolling her eyes. "Besides, this isn't the first time I've walked in with your wife's head between your legs, so don't pretend to be scandalized."

Marina caught Grace's eye, a question in her eyes. Grace shook her head. Marina's eyes widened and nodded towards Arthur.

"What are you two up to now?" Arthur asked, rubbing his temple. "And no more talk about what goes on in my sister's bedchamber."

Grace cupped her husband's cheek. "Well, my love, I have something to tell you."

He eyed her curiously. "Go on," he urged.

She grabbed his hand and placed it on her stomach, smiling at him. "You shall be a father."

Arthur pulled her close to him, placing sweet kisses all over her lips and face.

"Congratulations, brother," Marina said. "I'm so happy for you both!"

Grace giggled when Arthur lifted her and set her bottom on the edge of his desk. "Sister, I love you dearly and you can congratulate us later, but I need you to leave now and lock the door."

Marina smiled at them both and turned on her heel, for once doing as her brother requested. Grace shivered when the cool air reached her sensitive area after Arthur raised her skirts.

He flashed her a wicked grin. "My turn."

The Unlikely
Betrothal Series

Did you enjoy the banter between Arthur and his sister, Marina? Evan and Marina, Lord and Lady Ockham, are the hosts of the house party in my Unlikely Betrothal series!

Here is a look at the full series, and you can add them to your lists!

Visit https://christinadianebooks.com/ to learn more!

The Unlikely Betrothal Series

A different couple at the same house party finds their match! Who will be next? Each of these books are standalone stories complete with a HEA and lots of spice, but recommended reading order is below:

Book 1: The Earl and the Vixen

Book 2: The Rake and the Muse

Book 3: The Marquess and the Earl

Book 4: The Viscount and the Wallflower

Book 5: The Duke and the Widow

Dearest Reader

Thank you for taking the time to read Only A Rake Will Do! I hope that you enjoyed this short, spicy read!

I am so thankful to all of my readers and would appreciate it if you would leave an honest review (Amazon, Goodreads, BookBub, etc.) of the book! Also, I'd love to stay in touch, so follow me on socials and be sure to keep an eye out for my newsletters!

If you are interested in being on my permanent ARC team and/or Street Team, send me a message on one of my socials! I'd love to chat!

I hope all of you will follow me and get the latest happenings and info on releases from my historical romance friends on any of my socials:

- Website: christinadianebooks.com

- Instagram: @christinadianeauthor

- Facebook: christinadiane

- TikTok: @christinadianeauthor

- YouTube: @ChristinaDianeAuthor

- Twitter: @CDianeAuthor

- GoodReads: ChristinaDiane

- Follow Me onBookBub: Christina Diane

- Join my Reader Group: The Swoonworthy Scoundrels Society

- Join my other Author Group: Society of Smut & Scandal

Hopefully I left you wanting more, so be sure to continue reading to check out the first chapter of *The Earl and the Vixen*, book one in my Unlikely Betrothal series! I hope you are as excited as I am for Nick and Eliza! You can also go ahead and get your copy of The Earl and the Vixen: https://books2read.com/t heearlandthevixen

CHRISTINA
DIANE

The Earl and the Vixen - Chapter 1

Surrey, England - Spring 1811

"I love you, Eliza, and I intend to marry you. To hell with our fathers. Please tell me you want to be with me as much as I wish to be with you. In every way."

Elizabeth Nelson, the eldest daughter of the Earl of Nelson, melted into the arms of her sweetheart, Nicholas, who would one day become the Earl of Craven. She had loved him from the first time she'd come across him swimming in the stream that ran between their fathers' estates, almost five years ago.

Although the ownership of that very stream had been a long-disputed issue between their fathers. They each believed that the stream belonged to them and made trouble for each other when either household made use of it for livestock or to provide irrigation to crops. Ultimately, they both ended up using it for their estates anyway, and one would think they could be content with that. But a silly stream had been enough to cause such a rift that the men had sworn to hate each other. The bad blood only became worse between the pair over the years.

When she first saw Nick all those years ago, he hadn't given one whit about her back then. She had been far too young, and he had only been home for the summer from Eton, and by the time fall came again, he was gone. When he returned years later, he came across her reading a novel by the very same stream and finally noticed her, a woman and no longer an annoying young chit. They spent the next few months falling more in love each day and taking a few scandalous swims together at night in the stream in a rebellious slight against their fathers.

There wasn't a doubt in her mind that she wished to marry him, and she wanted nothing more than to give him every part of herself. To truly become his and make him hers. As a young woman of eight-and-ten whom no one spoke of such things to, she knew very little of what that would mean, but she knew she only wished to experience such things with Nick.

He would have offered to marry her already, and they would already be betrothed if they knew for certain how their fathers would react. Given the hatred the men harbored for each other, they feared that Eliza's father wouldn't agree to the union. With her age, they needed his approval to do so properly, or they would have to do something scandalous like elope to Gretna Green.

"I love you, too," she said, burying her face in his neck. "I want very much to be with you, Nick."

He took her mouth with his, kissing her with fervent intensity. When he broke the kiss, he brought her hands to his swollen lips. "Meet me at the hunting cabin tonight, after it is dark. We can be alone there, just the two of us with no one to disturb us."

She looked at their hands, attempting to mask her frown.

"What is it, Eliza? If you have doubts, we can wait," Nick said. He lifted her chin to meet his mesmerizing green eyes. His chestnut hair was just a bit longer than was fashionable, and it made him all the more roguish and handsome. "Look at me. I mean it, if this isn't something you wish to do—"

"It's not that," she said, cutting him off.

"Then is it something I have done? Did you not enjoy when I touched you..." his voice trailed off as he gestured towards her skirts.

"It is most certainly not that either," she said before swallowing hard. She had quite enjoyed it when he introduced her to the most exquisite pleasure she had ever experienced. "It's just that I know you have experienced these things before, and I haven't a clue what to expect or what to do."

Nick had always been honest with her, and he told her of his time at Cambridge and that there had been women who warmed his bed. He spared her the details, which she appreciated, but she wasn't so secure in herself that it didn't spark a flicker of jealousy, especially when she was about to lay herself bare before him.

She knew that the rules of society were different for men than women, especially since Nick was two-and-twenty and exposed to the things men do while at university, but it didn't mean she had to like it.

He cupped her cheek with his hand. "My love, you will be perfect. All I need is you. The rest we can explore together."

"But you—"

"Nothing that happened before you matters," he said, cutting her off, "and I know it isn't fair for me to say so, but I would be driven mad if I had to imagine even the mere notion of another man touching you. If I could change the past, I promise you, I would. Just know that it is of little import to me. You are my future. My everything."

She pressed onto her toes and kissed him again. "I will meet you tonight. I shall have to wait until after Papa goes to bed if I hope to leave." Her papa would not approve of her sneaking out to meet any man, let alone the son of the Earl of Craven. He might have apoplexy if he knew she intended to give Nick her virtue. Papa tolerated Nick's presence when he came to call only because of the politeness society expected. She was certain Papa would refuse him if it wouldn't upset Eliza. Perhaps when she and Nick married, their fathers might resolve things between them. One could only hope.

He brought her hand to his lips again and kissed her knuckles. "You had better return home before someone comes looking for us," he said. "I will see you tonight, my love."

She took his lips again for a few quick pecks and peeked around the corner from the back of her family's stables, ensuring no one could see her as she hurried back towards the house. Her father might tolerate Nick visiting for tea, but if he caught her with him unchaperoned, she wasn't certain she'd see the light of day again. They had to get creative to find ways to sneak off without her maid in tow.

Eliza made it back to the terrace of her grand country home without anyone taking notice. As soon as she entered, she almost walked straight into her father.

"Where have you been, daughter?" he asked.

"I was just taking in the air in the garden, Papa," she lied. She didn't enjoy lying to her father, but she couldn't have him locking her away in her room. Surely love was a reason to justify the minor sin.

His brow furrowed, assessing her. "Where is your maid? You shouldn't be roaming the grounds alone."

"You are quite right, Papa. I just stepped out for a few moments after I was tired of reading. I will make sure Dot goes with me next time," she said, hoping her father wouldn't press her any further.

"Very well. See that you do. Did that boy call here today?"

"Nick?" she asked.

Her father nodded. "And shouldn't you refer to him as Lord Craven?" Hate spewed when her father spoke the title. "You aren't on familiar terms."

Eliza opted not to point out that her father should also refer to Nick by his title and not "that boy," but she opted to leave that unsaid. "Papa, he isn't his father and has done nothing to you. And no, he didn't," she replied. It wasn't exactly a lie since he didn't come calling to their door. "Perhaps he will come for tea tomorrow."

"You are to depart for town with your mama in a few weeks for the season. You are certain to marry before the season ends, so there isn't much point in the boy calling here, I should think," he said, his lips curled into a smirk.

"Perhaps he will offer for me and save you the expense of a season, Papa," she said, testing the waters for her father's reaction.

If she hoped to find a hint of his thoughts on her statement, she would be disappointed. His expression remained unchanged, other than a slight squint of his eyes.

"Perhaps," he said, "but you would have many acceptable options if you had a season."

She patted her father's arm. "The most important thing is that I marry someone who loves me, right, Papa?"

"And someone who is respectable and comes from an excellent family. Someone who would ensure you are provided for," her father said, his cool expression still unchanged.

"Of course, Papa," she replied. "I should like to return to the new book I just purchased with my pin money. May I be excused?" She wasn't ready to tell her father she had already made her choice and would marry Nick. Even if she had to run away with him to

Gretna, he was the man she would marry, and there wasn't a thing her father could do about it.

"See you at dinner," her father said before departing towards his study.

Eliza continued to her room, unable to concentrate on reading as her heart wouldn't stop racing. She couldn't wait for her rendezvous with Nick later that evening, where she would learn what it meant to couple with the man she loved.

Around eleven o'clock, Eliza poked her head out of her room to see if anyone was lurking in the hallway. Dot had dressed her for bed a couple hours ago and set her hair into a long plait held in place with a ribbon before she sent the maid away for the evening. Eliza slipped on a serviceable day dress over her night rail and then covered herself with a pelisse to help keep from catching a chill in the cool night air.

Once she was certain there was no one moving about the house, she slipped out of her room and closed the door behind her. She made her way downstairs and snuck out via the door the servants used to access the kitchen garden.

The hunting cabin was only a ten-minute swift ride away, and she knew the route well. With a confident smile, she set off on the journey, assured of her safety under the luminous full moon. She crept to the mews, and a groom greeted her.

"Please saddle up my horse and tell no one that you saw me," she said, handing him a couple of coins.

He pocketed the coins and set off to do as she asked. Jimmy had done so for her a few times before, when she would sneak out to see Nick. The last time they snuck to the hunting cabin, she learnt what an orgasm was. Who knew that a man's hands could give such pleasure? She clenched her thighs together, already thinking about what delights he would introduce her to that evening.

A few moments later, Jimmy handed her the reins, positioning the horse by the mounting block. She thanked him and climbed into the saddle before flicking the reins and racing off into the night.

When she reached the cabin, Nick's horse was already tied up outside. He waited on the porch for her and came right beside her horse and lifted her down. "I'm so very glad you made it, my love. I would have preferred to escort you," Nick said, pulling her into an embrace for a quick kiss. "Let's get you inside. I already started a fire for us."

She grabbed his hand, and he led her inside. The warmth from the fire kissed her skin right away. She removed her pelisse and laid it across the back of the settee. She turned to face him, and in a single fluid movement, he swept her into his arms. Nick pressed his lips to hers, running his tongue along her bottom lip before her lips parted and he massaged her tongue with his. She returned his kiss, sucking his tongue into her mouth until he groaned.

He ambled her backward towards the bedchamber, not breaking their kiss, which grew wilder by the moment. Once inside the room, he kissed her jaw and neck, nibbling at her and then soothing the nips with his tongue.

Eliza sighed, loving the man before her more than she could have thought possible. She glanced around the room and noted he had started a fire in the bedchamber as well, and there were a few candles lit on the mantle above the fireplace.

Nick took her hands in his and leaned back to look at her. His expression was an intoxicating mixture of need and love, and with the light from fire casting shadows on his handsome face, it was an image depicted right out of one of her romance novels. His chestnut hair was almost black in the low lighting and the candlelight hit his green eyes just perfectly so that they shone like a precious gem. She lost her heart to him all over again.

"Are you certain you wish to do this?" he asked, placing a soft kiss on her jaw.

"More than anything," she replied. They had talked about waiting until they were married, but the desire to be with him had consumed her. She couldn't wait for her father to approve her choice. She needed to be with him in every way, and then they would fight for their future together.

A low growl escaped his lips, and he began working the buttons of her dress, unfastening enough that he could lift it over her head and then tossed it on the chair beside the bed.

Curious about what Nick would look like without his clothing, she unbuttoned the coat he wore and pushed it off his shoulders until it fell to the floor. She worked the buttons of his white shirt next. He remained still and allowed her to do as she wished, staring into her eyes as she undid each button and freed him from his shirt.

Her breath caught when she saw his muscular chest with a light smattering of dark hair. When she ran her hands across chiseled muscles and over his shoulders, he sucked in a breath, and the nerves she had about coupling with him evaporated, leaving only raw desire. She kissed his chest, becoming wanton and bold with each press of her lips to his skin. She used her tongue in the same way he did against her neck, and his muscles flexed beneath her touch.

"Eliza, that feels so good."

She licked and kissed his collarbone and up his neck, finding the lobe of his ear. She sucked it into her mouth.

He grabbed her head and kissed her lips again. After a few moments of exploration with their tongues, he broke the kiss and pulled her night rail over her head, leaving her naked before him.

She watched his response to her, and the hunger in his eyes only emboldened her further.

"You are so beautiful," he said, looking from her breasts and down her body. "I must taste you."

She wasn't sure what he meant, but he clasped her bottom and lifted her onto the bed. He tenderly laid her down across the massive bed and positioned himself on his knees between her legs.

He kissed her lips, then kissed his way to her breasts. Her entire body shivered from the sensation of his powerful form hovering over her and the anticipation of what he would do. She gasped when he took one of her nipples into his mouth and began suckling her. "Nick," she cried out.

"Do you like this?" he asked, stopping what he was doing.

"Oh, yes," she replied.

He dipped his head to continue, smiling against her breast every time she moaned or sucked in a breath. When he used his hand to find her nub in the nest of curls between her legs, she moaned again.

He released her nipple and kissed his way down her stomach. He kissed lower and lower, shifting himself further down on the bed until his head was between her legs.

"What are you—" She cried out when his tongue flicked her pearl. "God, yes," she moaned.

He stopped and glanced up at her, a smirk playing on his lips. "Does that mean you wish for me to continue?"

"I may never wish for you to stop."

He gave a smug laugh and flicked her pearl again before circling it with his tongue. He inserted a finger into her core and moved it in and out. Her hands flew to his head, and she undulated against his mouth and hand.

She approached a release similar to the one he gave her a couple of nights ago with his hand, but this was different. Far more intense and wicked. When she tipped over the edge of her climax, she rocked and moaned, calling out his name.

He shifted himself on top of her and kissed her lips. She tasted herself on his tongue and licked the wetness off his lips. It was erotic and exhilarating, and she knew that once would never be enough.

"I could drink from you all day," he said.

"I may wish for you to do just that." She giggled when he laughed at her declaration. "I didn't know such a thing was possible," she said.

He kissed her again. "Would you like to stop now, or would you like for me to show you more?"

"I want more," she replied, the need evident in her tone. "Please, Nick."

Nick climbed off the bed and stood beside it, looking at her.

"Where are you going?" she asked, curving her lips in a playful pout.

"I must remove these now," he replied, working the buttons of his falls, his eyes not leaving hers. He pushed his breeches down to the floor and his member sprang to life, protruding from a nest of dark curls. Her gaze fixed on it, curious about what it might feel like in her hand.

He climbed back onto the bed and hovered over her, placing another sweet kiss on her lips.

"I want to touch you," she said, reaching between them to grasp the rod that stood erect between them.

He sucked in a large breath and closed his eyes when her hand closed around it. Balancing himself with one hand and his knees, he reached his free hand between them and wrapped it around hers. His cock was smooth to the touch but hard as steel.

"You can stroke me like this." He moved her hand with his, and she loved the power she felt from giving him pleasure the way he did for her.

She continued to stroke him for a few moments before he pulled her hand away. "I will spend if you should continue, and I would much rather do so after I make you come on my cock."

She bit her lip, enjoying his wicked words. "Tell me what you are going to do and don't be polite about it."

He slipped his hand between them and slid two fingers inside of her. "I'm going to replace my fingers with the head of my aching shaft, and then I'm going to move like this"—he slid his fingers in and out—"until you shatter and moan in my arms."

She released a sound that was a mixture of a sign and a moan. He pressed his lips to her ear. "Do you want me inside you now?" he whispered.

She nodded.

"Tell me you want me to make love to you with my needy cock," he said, kissing along her jaw.

"I want your cock, Nick," she whispered. "Make love to me. Now."

He withdrew his fingers and positioned himself at her opening. "This may hurt but not for long, and it shouldn't do so ever again."

He pushed himself into her with care, inch by inch. She gasped from the slight twinge of pain when he had his entire length inside of her.

"Are you all right?" he asked.

"Yes," she whispered, the pain subsiding, and she had the urge to move against him. "It doesn't hurt any longer."

He withdrew and then thrust back inside of her, causing her to see stars. She had never imagined such a pleasure and reveled in the intimacy from the man she loved most in the world filling her, the two of them joining as one. Nothing and no one else mattered but the two of them. He did it again, and she cried out.

"That's it, my love. Moan as loud as you wish. It drives me wild to hear you do so."

With every moan, he thrust deeper and harder inside of her. She wrapped her legs around him, and it became even more intense when he entered her as far as he could. He panted and groaned, and she pushed herself against him to meet his thrusts.

"You are mine," he said, thrusting hard and deep.

She responded with a loud moan and dug her fingers into his back.

"Say it," he whispered against her lips.

Eliza kissed him and broke the kiss to speak. "I am yours," she said. "I shall always be yours."

He thrust into her harder and faster.

"Oh, yes," she cried out. "Just like that. Don't stop." With each movement, she neared ever closer to madness and ecstasy. "Nick," she moaned.

He didn't relent and made good on his promise to make her shatter. When she did, she cried out his name again and bucked beneath him, arching her back. Once she rode every wave of the intense pleasure from her climax, he withdrew, his breath ragged. "God, Eliza," he groaned before warm liquid pooled on her stomach.

After a few moments, Nick climbed from the bed and removed a handkerchief from his pocket. He wiped between her legs, then her stomach, and set the handkerchief on the table beside the bed.

"I wiped away the blood, but you may be sore tomorrow. A warm bath should help," he said, settling in next to her and pulling her into his arms.

"That was more wonderful than I imagined," she said, brushing his hair away from his face. "I hope it was the same for you."

He pulled her tighter against him. "My love, I have never experienced anything as intense as being with you. I fear I am addicted to you and shall never get enough."

She giggled beside him. "Is that so?"

"It's perfect since you are mine," he said, kissing her forehead.

"Does that mean you shall meet me here tomorrow night and show me more?" she asked, placing a quick kiss on his chest.

"Nothing on this earth could keep me away."

Acknowledgments

There are so many amazing people in my life who have supported me, new and old. Authors and readers! I truly appreciate each and every one of you and hope that you will continue to stick with me on this journey. I would like to call out a few key people, but please know that this isn't an exhaustive list and there are so many people whom I love and adore. I wish that I had room to name them all!

Steve: My husband is the one who continually supports my big and daring dreams, all while providing tech support, cooking dinner, doing the laundry, spitballing ideas with me, and so much more! He's a true partner in every extent of the word and I couldn't do any of it without him. Love you, Babe!

Dexter and Felix: My boys frequently provide me with distractions while I'm in the middle of writing. However, they are also often the inspiration for some of the witty sibling banter that makes it into my drafts. I don't even know what they're going to think when they realize one day that their mother writes smut. Oh well... I love you, boys!

Rachel, Nina & Brittany: I am fortunate to have these ladies (my mom, aunt, and sister) in my life. They have been there for me the entire way and have supported me through the ups and downs throughout the years. They are all used to my crazy ideas and what I can do when I put my mind to something. They just keep cheering me on. They are the ones who hold all of my embarrassing stories and memories, so I can't ever let anyone speak to them without me present. But I love you, all!

Erin: We were destined to be besties from our very first meeting. She is the person I talk to about all the things when I need to bounce around ideas, work on my mindset, take a breath, and so much more! Love you, dearly!

Morgan: None of this could be possible without her keeping the trains moving! If there is something with this biz that needs to get done, she is right there at my side helping move it forward, and she usually comes up with a simpler, better idea! Truly, thank you!!!

Bliss: I can't believe the good fortune we had to have met in a smutty follow train group on Insta, but here we are! It was another fateful moment! I would be sad without our daily texts, talking about our writing progress, smutty scenes, and all the happenings in life. Thank you so much!!!

Courtney: Fate struck again, and I am so thankful to have a partner in crime and twinsie for this author journey! Thanks for all of the ideating, chats, and feedback into the wee hours of the morning! We are going to rock this thing!

Thank you to everyone on my Beta, ARC, and Street Team! (Especially Rachel W., she has literally read every single word that I have written, and I haven't scared her away yet!) The love and care that you put into reading, providing feedback, and helping promote the stories means so much more to me than you know. I hope we get to keep hanging out together for many years to come!

Thank you to Dragonblade Publishing for seeing something in me and my stories! I know I am going to continue to grow in my author career with your guidance and support.

Thank you to all of the amazing author friends and influencers I have met through various social media groups! This amazing community has seriously been one of the best parts of this whole journey, and I am thankful you all let me be a part of it!

Meet The Author

Christina Diane is an award-winning, internationally bestselling author who loves to write super spicy, fast paced stories for the modern reader in the genres of historical romance and dark romance. Her historical romances are all set in the Regency era, with creative liberty taken within the historical setting to create a passionate, hot, intriguing story. Across all of her works, if you love combinations of high spice, witty banter, spirited heroines, forbidden romances, darker themes, and hot alpha men...then you are in for a treat! Because bad boys never go out of style!

She is a hybrid indie and traditionally published author with Dragonblade Publishing, Romance Cafe, and And You Press. She reads mostly spicy Regency romances and all shades of dark romances, as well as thrillers.

Christina lives in Northern Maine with her husband and two boys. Her family also includes their three French bulldogs who go everywhere with them, as well as two solid black cats. The entire family is always up for new adventures. When she is not writing or chasing after her family, she usually has a Kindle in her hand!

Her writing journey began at the age of nine when she created her own comic strip, Grizzly Grouch. In adulthood, she was a freelance writer for several years, mostly writing lifestyle pieces for blogs. She found that she couldn't stop thinking about stories and characters, so much that she had to get them on the page! Christina frequently has dreams of random character ARCs that go into a massive list of planned writings. She currently has more than ten series just waiting to be written!

Aside from her family, writing, and books, she loves *Bridgerton*, the Grinch, Jessica Rabbit, horror movies, Chucky dolls, cold brew, yoga, *Hamilton*, the color pink, and speaking in obscure quotes from movies and TV shows.

Christina loves chatting with her readers and talking about great reads, so please contact her on socials! She'd love to hear what you think about her books and what you'd love to see more of!